WHERE'S THE CAT?

Stella Blackstone & Debbie Harter

ABBEVILLE KIDS
A Division of Abbeville Publishing Group
New York London Paris

First published in Great Britain in 1996 by Barefoot Books Ltd.

First published in the United States of America in 1996 by
Abbeville Press, 488 Madison Avenue, New York, NY 10022.

Text copyright © 1996 by Stella Blackstone
Illustrations copyright © 1996 by Debbie Harter

Graphic design: DW Design, London

Printed and bound in Belgium

First edition
10 9 8 7 6 5 4 3 2 1

ISBN 0-7892-0290-5

where's
the cat?

on the chair

where's
the cat?

up
the
stair

where's
the cat?

under the bed

where's
the cat?

behind
the shed

where's
the cat?

under the coat

where's
the cat?

where's
the cat?

up the tree

where's
the cat?

where's
the cat?

in the hall

where's
the cat?

with the ball

where's
the cat?